SWEETER THAN EVER

~ The Sullivans Honeymoon Novella ~

Smith and Valentina Sullivan

Bella Andre

4/17

SWEETER THAN EVER
~ The Sullivans Honeymoon Novella ~
Smith and Valentina Sullivan
© 2017 Bella Andre

Sign up for Bella's New Release Newsletter
www.BellaAndre.com/newsletter
bella@bellaandre.com
www.BellaAndre.com
Bella on Twitter: @bellaandre
Bella on Facebook: facebook.com/bellaandrefans

Millions of readers around the world have fallen in love with the Sullivans—especially Smith Sullivan, the movie star with the heart of gold. Get ready to join Smith and his new wife, Valentina, as they embark on their life together with the sweetest, sexiest, most surprising honeymoon ever. Just-wedded bliss that will sizzle, make you laugh out loud...and tug on your heartstrings. After all, true love—and family—are what the Sullivans do best!

A note from Bella

I had so much fun writing the double wedding in *Every Beat of My Heart*—and so many wonderful readers wrote to tell me how much you enjoyed catching up with your favorite Sullivans—that I knew I wanted to write many more Sullivan novellas in the future!

I've always had a soft spot for Smith Sullivan, the hero of *Come A Little Bit Closer,* the seventh book set in San Francisco. Not only is Smith a sexy and brilliantly talented man, he is also devoted to his family. Getting to spend more time with one of my favorite couples on their romantic, funny, and very sexy honeymoon was such a gift. I hope you enjoy catching up with them as much as I have!

If this is your first time reading about the Sullivans, you can easily read each book as a stand-alone—and there is a Sullivan family tree available on my website (bellaandre.com/sullivan-family-tree) so you can see how the books connect together!

Happy reading,
Bella Andre

P.S. Many more Sullivan love stories are coming soon! Please be sure to sign up for my newsletter (bellaandre.com/newsletter) so that you don't miss out on any announcements.

And I can't wait for you to learn more about their friends, Calvin Vaughn and Christie Hayden, from Summer Lake! Calvin's very emotional and sexy second chance love story—*The Best Is Yet To Come*—will be released May 2017. And Christie's breathtaking romance with the one man she never expected to fall in love with—*Can't Take My Eyes Off Of You*—will be released July 2017.

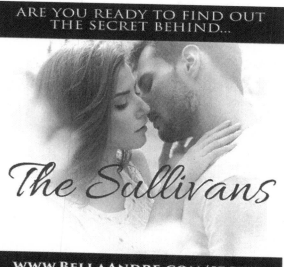

ARE YOU READY TO FIND OUT
THE SECRET BEHIND...

The Sullivans

WWW.BELLAANDRE.COM/SECRET

CHAPTER ONE

Smith Sullivan was the luckiest guy in the world.

Just hours earlier, he'd pledged his forever love to Valentina Landon in front of their family and friends in an intimate wedding ceremony at Summer Lake. She'd given him her heart, all of it—the light, the dark, the whole, the broken, the sweet, the edgy—and he would never stop being amazed by his wife.

Wife.

No word had ever been sweeter.

Smith had waited thirty-six years for her, and hadn't actually thought a woman existed who wouldn't want him only for his fame, his success, his money. But Valentina had blown away every worry, every fear.

The moment he'd met her, back when she was still managing her sister Tatiana's acting career, he'd known. Valentina was special.

From the first look, the first word she'd spoken, the first time she'd touched him, kissed him—she'd gotten beneath his skin. Down to the real Smith Sullivan that he rarely let anyone but his family see.

She hadn't wanted him to woo her, hadn't wanted anything to do with an actor, had been horrified at the thought of ending up in the spotlight. But he hadn't been able to let her go. There was no fight he wouldn't fight for her. No lengths he wouldn't go to prove his love to her. He wanted her with a passion that ran so deep, so true, it rocked his world every time they made love.

Miracle of miracles, she felt exactly the same way about him.

"There it is." He pointed through the trees to the cabin in the woods where they were going to spend their honeymoon.

"It's perfect." She squeezed his hand, and the smile she gave him lit him up from the inside out. "I love you."

"I love you too." And he was dying to be alone with her.

Completely alone for once.

Between the time they spent with their families— they had nearly enough relatives around the world to fill a stadium with a family reunion—and the casts and crews of the films they wrote, produced, and directed, they were constantly surrounded by people. People they liked a great deal, fortunately, but it still meant that the two of them didn't get nearly enough time alone.

One week together in the Maine woods felt like the greatest gift possible. And he wanted to make the most of every single second.

Smith worked to tamp down his impatience by reminding himself that the flight on his private jet from the Adirondack Mountains of New York into the Bangor, Maine, airport had been smooth and fast. Traffic on the road heading toward the cabin had been lighter than usual, as if the other drivers knew not to mess with the newlyweds tonight. The cabin's windows and porch light glowed in the darkness, making the cabin look as though it belonged in a fairy tale.

Everything was perfect so far. But it was going to be so much better once he had Valentina inside the cabin. Once he could strip away her clothes and show her with his body what he'd said with his wedding vows. Yes, he knew they were going to have a lifetime together, but he'd still been wanting her, needing her more and more with every second that had passed since the ceremony.

He pulled their rental car up beside the cottage, turned off the ignition, then jumped out and quickly moved to the passenger side to yank open the door and scoop Valentina into his arms.

She looked slightly dazed by how fast he'd reached her when she'd barely undone her seat belt. "On our first night together," she said in a soft voice as she wound her arms around his neck, "you did the same thing after we returned from Alcatraz."

"All I wanted was to make you mine." He kissed her, stealing one tempting taste that wasn't nearly enough to make a dent in his desire. "Now you are. *Finally.*"

"I've always been yours. From the first moment we met, you've had my heart."

As he took her mouth again, he was tempted, so damned tempted to lay her down on the bed of pine needles beneath the tall trees and make love to her. With only the night sky and the smell of the nearby ocean around them.

Only, he knew better. Knew that for someone in his profession, with his level of fame, there might be a drone watching, filming, intruding, no matter the safeguards he'd put in place. He didn't believe in wasting his life moaning about the difficulties of living in the spotlight, and neither did Valentina, but right about now, he damn well wasn't happy about them either.

Kicking the car door shut, he took long strides toward the cabin's entrance. Toward the utter and total privacy that they would have once they were inside. He already knew they wouldn't make it to the bedroom, that they'd be ripping off each other's clothes as soon as he locked the door behind them.

God, he couldn't *wait*. Even the thirty seconds remaining between putting the key into the lock and shoving the door open felt like an interminably long time.

Smith didn't so much as glance at the interior of the cabin before closing the door, turning the lock, and lowering his mouth back to Valentina's. The way her tongue slipped and slid against his—and the little sounds of pleasure she was making—told him that she was just as eager for these seven precious days and nights with just the two of them to begin.

He swore time slowed as he slid her down the length of his body and pressed her back against the door. Her hazel eyes had gone a dark green with desire. Her golden skin was infused with a rosy glow of passion. And her breath was coming as fast as his.

She was beautiful in a navy striped top and jeans, the clothes she'd changed into after their wedding reception for their trip to Maine. He made a mental note to replace them after their honeymoon as he took a fistful of cotton in each hand and prepared to tear her shirt off.

"Smith?" The voice—a very unexpected one—came from behind them. The woman cleared her throat. "Valentina?"

Smith barely bit back the curse about to fly from his lips. Valentina, though also clearly frustrated by having the lovemaking they'd both been dying for interrupted, put her hand on his cheek and gave him one more soft kiss, before stepping out from behind him with a smile on her face.

"Cassie." She headed toward the kitchen, her arms outstretched as she met Smith's cousin for a hug. "Thank you so much for offering to let us stay in your cabin for our honeymoon."

"It's my pleasure," Cassie said, looking sincerely apologetic and more than a little embarrassed. "And can I just say how stupendously sorry I am that I didn't get out of here before you arrived? I shouldn't have parked my car around back. At least then you would have known I was still here."

Smith needed a couple of seconds to deal with his frustration, before finally turning around and going over to give his cousin a bear hug.

Over her shoulder, he finally noticed what a great job she'd done setting up the cabin for them. There was an enormous vase of lilies of the valley on the dining room table, a flower that held deep meaning for them, along with a chilling bottle of champagne and several other bottles of wine, a huge bowl of fresh fruit, and countless other touches meant to make the newlyweds feel completely at home.

"You didn't need to go to all this trouble, Cassie." That was when it hit him. "You must have left the wedding early to come back to do this for us."

"I wanted everything to be perfect for you. Which should have included," she said with a wry grin, "your cousin not being here to kill the mood. So on that note—" She headed back into the kitchen to pick up her bag. "—I'll say congratulations one more time, and wish you both a very happy honeymoon."

"Don't go yet," Valentina said. "We don't see nearly enough of you. Stay awhile longer. Please."

Cassie looked at Smith, her silent question clear: *Are you sure you can handle some more family time right now?*

But that was the thing: Smith hadn't just fallen for Valentina because of her exotic beauty. He hadn't just gone head over heels for her because of her incredible intelligence and talent. Nor was it simply that she was hotter and wilder than anything he'd ever dreamed when they were making love.

He'd completely lost his heart to her because family meant as much to her as it did to him.

"Valentina's right—we haven't been able to catch up with you in far too long. Why don't we open a bottle of the wine you so thoughtfully brought, and then you can bring us up to date on everything." He was already working the corkscrew in as he asked, "How are things going with your candy business?"

"Good," she said as she went to get three wine

glasses from the cupboard. "Busy."

"I'm really glad to hear that," Valentina said as they headed into the living room, where Cassie had lit a fire for them. "You're so talented. I show everyone the pictures of the treasure chest you made for our last film, and no one can believe you spun it out of sugar."

As they sat on the couch, Valentina curled beneath his arm, warm and sweet smelling. Pushing back his impatience to be alone with her, he asked Cassie, "And what about that guy you were seeing?" He tried for the name, but came up blank.

"Trust me," his cousin said in a wry tone, "I've happily forgotten his name too. I'd much rather spend the night with a bunch of sugar than with him."

Smith was as protective of his cousins as he was of his sisters. "If he hurt you in any way—"

"No," she said with a shake of her head. "It was nothing." She frowned, taking a long drink from her glass, as if for sustenance. "We were just a bad fit. But my lackluster love life is most certainly not what you need to be talking about on your honeymoon. Especially after I just interrupted you two..." Her cheeks went pink. "You know, doing what newlyweds should be doing."

With that, she put her empty glass on the coffee table and stood. "I really do want to catch up, but tonight should be just for you. The whole week should. I've stocked the fridge, so you shouldn't need to go out for any meals or even to the grocery store if you don't want to."

Smith deeply appreciated that Cassie understood his life well enough to prepare them to go completely underground and off the radar for a full week.

His cousin gave Valentina a hug, then pressed a kiss to Smith's cheek. "Call me at the end of the week if you're up for a meal together. And if you're not," she added with a wink, "I won't be offended in the least."

When Valentina walked Cassie out to her car, Smith figured he might as well bring in their suitcases. That way there really wouldn't be any reason for them to leave the cabin again.

Smith Sullivan was a man with enough wealth and power to have anything he wanted. But seven days and seven nights of Valentina all to himself was priceless.

And he couldn't wait one more second to make Mrs. Valentina Sullivan *his*.

CHAPTER TWO

Valentina found Smith waiting for her inside—and her heart leaped in her chest just looking at him.

She could still hardly believe that he was hers—this incredible man, who had more love to give than anyone she'd ever known. It didn't hurt, of course, that he was also stupendously good looking. Tall, broad, chiseled. With a face so handsome, so sexy, it stopped hearts all over the world.

She licked her lips as he continued to stare at her from across the living room with that intensely sensual gaze that always melted her insides.

"Valentina."

As he moved toward her, she stood rooted in place. How could she possibly get her legs to work when it was taking everything she had just to think clearly? He was the only one who called her by her full name, rather than *Val*—and the way he said *Valentina* made every part of her heat up, head to toe.

"Finally," he said once he was standing before her, "we're alone."

She could hear the anticipation thrumming in his voice, just as she could feel it inside of her. Working on film sets where the hours often stretched from dawn until long after sundown meant that they had learned how to take advantage of any possible chance to be alone—even if it was just ten minutes stolen in an editing booth or a dressing room at a studio event. Seven days and nights alone together was the greatest wedding gift they could have given each other.

Finally, as his arms opened, she came unstuck. Putting her hands around his neck at the same time as he slid his around her waist, she looked up into his deep blue eyes and felt such joy that her grin beat out the kiss she'd been planning to give to her new husband.

Once upon a time, she'd been afraid to do this, to step into Smith's arms. The first time he'd asked her out, standing in her studio trailer on the *Gravity* film set in San Francisco, she'd so badly wanted to say yes. But all her baggage, her past hurts, had risen up inside of her, had filled her with panic. So she'd asked to just be friends. *"We already are,"* was what he'd told her.

And it was true. Smith wasn't just her wickedly sensual lover, wasn't just her husband whom she couldn't wait to spend the rest of her life with.

He was also her best friend.

His grin mirrored hers, and then he lowered his mouth to her ear and said, in a deep voice that had thrill bumps running all across her skin, "Remember the first time we made love?"

"God, yes." Her response was barely more than a whisper of need.

How could she possibly forget the way he'd loved her after they'd returned from a fairy-tale trip to Alcatraz? All the dreams of love that she'd been too scared to let herself dream had begun to come true that night.

"Tonight," he promised, "is going to be even better. Even sweeter. Even hotter."

He pressed a kiss to her neck, just below her earlobe, and she shivered at the delicious sensation of his mouth on her skin. It was yet another thing she knew she'd never get used to—Smith's lips, his hands, his body on hers. Every time he kissed her, every time he touched her, it was special. Perfect.

And so hot that need sizzled through her veins like molten lava.

Though it was nearly impossible to force herself to move out of his arms, she made herself step back, far enough that the only points of contact that remained were his hands on her hips. God, she loved how big, how rough, and also how gentle his hands were.

"I'm ready for you to unwrap me now."

Heat leaped even higher in his eyes as he lifted his hands to the leather laces that held the front of her navy striped shirt closed. She'd bought the top for these laces, hoping they would drive Smith crazy, making him desperate to tear them away to reveal what lay beneath.

He had been playing with the laces since they'd left their wedding reception, winding the leather around his fingers, almost absently. Although she knew he never did anything absently. It was one of the reasons he was such a great actor and director—he was fully present in any moment. And when they were making love...

Oh yes, Smith's ability to be so fully in the moment was a truly beautiful thing.

Now, instead of rushing, instead of ripping her shirt open, he rubbed the leather straps between thumb and forefinger. It felt like he was touching her instead, as though he was playing over the sensitive skin of her breasts rather than the leather.

Slowly—so slowly that she was already on the verge of begging—he began to slide the laces apart, revealing first one inch of skin at the top of her chest, and then another, and another after that. With each patch of skin he uncovered, he paused to stroke one fingertip lightly over her, so lightly that if she hadn't been so attuned to his every touch, his every move, his every breath, she might not have felt it.

"Soft." The word was barely more than a whisper

of sound, just like his caress. He lowered his head, then, and kissed the skin he'd just bared. "Sweet." He licked out over her skin, making her shiver at the heat, the sensuality, between them. He lifted his head and looked her in the eye. *"Mine."*

When he crushed her mouth beneath his, she welcomed his savage passion. Took every ounce of his desire and gave him back just as much.

Until Smith, she had always held in her emotions. She had been certain that it was the only way to stay safe, the only way to protect herself from future pain. But with Smith, she'd never been able to hold herself back. Not when their chemistry was this extraordinary, this inevitable.

And not when she trusted him with every part of her heart.

Desire and joy were a wonderful jumble inside of her by the time he lifted his lips from hers.

She reached out to stroke his jaw, dark now with stubble from the long, beautiful day they'd had, then looked down at her still intact shirt. "Yours *and* ready for more unwrapping."

"All day," he said, "I've been fantasizing about what you're wearing beneath your clothes."

Her voice was husky as she told him, "I've been waiting all day for you to find out."

That was all it took for his control to snap. No

longer able to go slow and tease them both with heady anticipation, he gripped the open edges of her shirt and tore them apart, both the fabric and the leather shredding.

"You're a goddess, Valentina."

She felt her skin flush even hotter than it already was, simply from the burn in his eyes as he looked at her. She'd always had a weakness for beautiful lingerie. Which fit perfectly with Smith's weakness for buying it for her—the softest silk, the finest lace.

But she'd bought this set herself, knowing she would wear it on her wedding night, hoping that Smith would look at her just the way he was now. With awe. With wonder.

And with such hunger that her knees felt as though they'd turned to Jell-O.

He still hadn't reached for her, was simply staring as if he couldn't believe his eyes. "Where did you find this?"

She took his hands in hers, lifting them to the center of her chest, where her heart was beating out a wild rhythm. "Italy. In the town next to the one where your mother was born. She told me about an old friend of hers, a seamstress who specializes in lace and silk. She promised me it would be the most beautiful thing I'd ever have against my skin. But she was wrong." His eyes lifted with surprise to hers, and a moment later she said, "You are."

At last, his hands came alive with a gentle caress over the cream-colored fabric that had literally been sewn onto her body as she'd stood in the seamstress's twelfth-century workroom months earlier.

All day, as she'd felt it brushing against her curves, she'd imagined it was Smith's hands instead. So clearly that she'd driven herself half-mad with longing during the long wait through the wedding and reception and the flight to Maine. Waiting for precisely this moment when he finally saw her lace and silk gift-wrapping.

And stripped it away.

His strong hands trembled as he moved his thumbs beneath the whisper-thin silk straps over her shoulders. She held her breath as he slowly slid them off. The swells of her breasts rose higher beneath the sheer lace that—just barely now—still covered her. Her heart was pounding hard enough that she wondered if Smith could see it flutter just beneath the surface of her skin.

He lowered his mouth to her again, first to one bared shoulder, and then the other, before he found her beating pulse with a kiss that was so reverent, so loving, she had to reach out for his forearms to keep herself upright.

Lifting his head, he traced the fine line where lace met skin once, then twice, until she was making little pleading sounds that could have only one meaning.

More. She wanted him to take more of her. To take *all* of her.

And then—finally—he undid the fine thread of silk that held the lace together. As the silk thread slid apart, the beautiful bra fell away.

Smith didn't say a word, but he didn't have to because his mouth, his hands were already saying everything Valentina longed to hear. His tongue teased, his fingers tantalized. Even the scrape of dark stubble on his chin across her aroused skin was almost more sensation than she could bear. She arched into him, gave herself completely over to soul-deep pleasure.

Again and again, he laved her breasts, first one and then the other, until the arousal rolling through her was so intense that she literally couldn't stay on her feet.

He lifted her in his arms, his mouth devouring hers as he strode out of the living room, past the kitchen, and down the hall. The next thing she knew, she was on the bed and he was moving over her. He looked savage, his control hanging by only the barest thread.

She nearly wept with joy when he all but tore her shoes and jeans from her. Only to stop for a few breathless moments so that he could marvel at the gorgeous panties that covered her hips, a match to the lace and silk of the hand-sewn bra.

"Beautiful."

Despite his desperation, he was careful not to tear the delicate fabric as he slid it down her thighs. And then, she was bared to him. Completely open to his gaze. To his touch. To *him*.

"So damned beautiful."

He was seemingly everywhere at once. At her breasts, between her thighs, at her mouth. With his muscular body over hers, pressing her deeper into the mattress, he kissed and licked and laved and caressed.

Hours of anticipation since their ceremony had stolen what little control she had, so when he stroked his fingers inside of her at the same moment that his lips closed over the taut tip of her breast, she shattered. Breaking into a million beautiful pieces with the man she had vowed to love forever.

A promise she'd made to him long before she'd worn a wedding gown and spoken the words aloud in front of their friends and family.

CHAPTER THREE

Smith had planned a slow seduction on their wedding night. He'd wanted to spin Valentina so high with pleasure—up and up and up and up—that by the time he claimed her with his body, she would be utterly consumed by the force of her need, her desire.

But he was a fool. Because going slow would mean that he was in control. And the truth was that he'd never had an ounce of self-control around her—less now that she was his wife than ever before.

Again and again, as he'd run kisses over her body, he kept flashing back to seeing her walk down the aisle toward him earlier that day in her elegant wedding dress. The sun had shone through her veil, the breeze lifting it to tease him with glimpses of her stunning face, her expression alight with the same joy as his, her cheeks wet with tears, just as his were.

Valentina had been luminous. Breathtakingly beautiful.

His.

Their vows had cemented the promises they'd

made to each other already. Love. Devotion. Unconditional support. And beneath everything they'd spoken aloud in front of friends and family had been *this*.

This passion.

This desire.

This longing to be as close as they possibly could to one another.

For their arms and legs to tangle, their mouths to devour. For her pleasure to become his, and his to be hers.

Valentina was officially a Sullivan now. And Smith had never been happier in his life.

He needed to show her with more than words just what she meant to him. That she was more precious than anyone, anything else, could ever be.

He found her lips again with his, his kiss both rough and sweet, desire and love perfectly blended. She kissed him back with just as much fervor, and he loved how sensual she was in their private darkness, especially in contrast to what she let the rest of the world see. There was nothing he liked more than tangling her hair with his hands while they made love, to see it spread out across a pillow, her skin flushed with need, her mouth swollen from his kisses.

But he wasn't the only one who craved. Because as they kissed, she reached for his shirt, and with one fierce tug on cotton, she tore it open.

"Smith." He could hear the lingering pleasure from her climax in her voice, along with obvious impatience. "I need you. *Now.*"

"You have me. You always have."

Again they kissed, wild and desperate for each other, need shooting through his veins. The need to possess and be possessed. The need to claim and be claimed. The need to love each other face to face, chest to chest, hips to hips, as deeply connected as a man and woman could possibly be.

He helped her shove the rest of his clothes off. Once there was nothing left between them, he levered above her on his forearms and stared. Marveled at the most beautiful woman in the world lying beneath him.

His ring on her finger. Her ring on his.

"I love you."

Her mouth lifted at the corners, her smile lifting his heart as she said, "I love you too. So much, Smith. More than you'll ever know."

"I do know," he said as he gathered her in his arms and she put her arms and legs around him. "I know how much you love me, because I love you exactly the same way."

His final word was barely out when they both moved together, Valentina opening to him at the same moment he thrust deep.

"Valentina." Her name was a vow, a blessing, a

dream, as her heat, her arousal, surrounded him. Made it so that he couldn't think, could barely breathe, could only lose himself inside of her.

With her hands, her legs, her hips, her words, she urged him to take her. Harder. Faster. Wilder.

Every time they made love he was amazed by the sparks, the heat, the power they created between them. But no bliss, no ecstasy, had ever come close to this moment when he looked into her eyes and found her staring into his just as deeply, just as intensely.

Smith knew he'd never forget this evening—the way Valentina looked, smelled, sounded, tasted, felt. The way she gave every last part of herself over to him with total trust. And with joy.

Utterly lost in each other, the next wave of pleasure—bigger than any he'd ever felt before—lifted them high, sweeping them up in sensations so good, so true, that they had to cling to each other just to hold on. Had to try to pull oxygen from each other's lungs in something that was far beyond a kiss.

For long minutes after, they lay wrapped around each other working to catch their breath. Finally, she laughed, and when he lifted his head from her shoulder to look into her bright eyes, she said, "It's always been amazing, but never like *that*."

He couldn't help the proud grin that took over his

face. What guy could, when told he'd just fully and completely rocked his wife's world, even beyond what she'd thought was possible?

"We've just had the perfect beginning to what's going to be a perfect week," he told her. "No one will ever think to look for us here. Which means we have seven straight days to do that again and again and again."

"Sounds like the perfect honeymoon to me," she agreed.

He would happily have started all over again, but he couldn't miss the faint smudges beneath her eyes. Her yawn, one that seemed to surprise her, cemented his decision.

"Stay right where you are. I'll put together a tray of food to eat in bed, and then we're going to get some rest." His grin was wicked, as was the stroke of his hand over her curves. "Believe me, you're going to need to be well fed and rested for what I have planned for you."

"I can't wait," she said, even as she settled more deeply into the pillows, her eyes already fluttering closed.

Smith wasn't surprised to find her asleep by the time he came back in with the open bottle of wine, some crackers, cheese, and cold cuts. A midnight snack would be waiting if she woke, but for now all he wanted was to climb beneath the covers, pull her into his arms, and sleep together for the very first time as husband and wife.

CHAPTER FOUR

Valentina woke warm and cozy in Smith's arms, his front to her back like a spoon, the sound of rain pattering on the roof. She was utterly content, needing nothing more than this.

As a young girl, she'd believed she'd find a love like the one her parents had. Strong. True. But then, after her father died when she was twenty-two and her mother had gone off the rails by hooking up with one smarmy actor after another, Valentina had stopped believing. She'd gone into protective warrior mode to take care of her sister, Tatiana, and herself.

Valentina had never expected a man like Smith to come along. She'd sworn never to lose her heart to an actor, yet he was unlike any she'd ever met. He'd been gentle enough to soothe her. Strong enough to topple the walls she'd built up around herself. And steady enough not to give up when anyone else would have.

Love overflowed as she brought the arm he'd slung over her waist close to her heart. She felt him stir, felt his warm breath on her neck as he pressed a kiss to her nape.

She opened her mouth to say good morning, but the press of one strong thigh between hers stole her breath away and made it impossible to speak. He was rock hard behind her, from the muscles of his chest, abs, hips, and legs...to the erection that made her instantly grow damp and hot with need.

He lifted their linked hands over her shoulder so that he could kiss her knuckles, and then he let her hand go so that he could play over her skin with the flat of his palm.

As he stroked her, lingering at the swells of her breasts before brushing over her waist and then flaring out to her hips, she felt every inch a sensual woman. A naughty one who wanted nothing more than to be taken by her lover.

Her *husband*.

She turned her face to his and kissed him with all of the love in her heart. Just as their lips met, he slid his hand from her hip to the throbbing vee between her legs. On a moan against his mouth, she rolled her hips up into his touch. The gorgeous slide of his fingers over her. Into her.

She was already close, could have leaped off the edge into bliss with nothing more than the press of his talented fingers over her arousal, his lips against hers. But she wanted more.

She wanted *everything*.

There was something so sweet—and yet so wonderfully naughty—about their early-morning lovemaking. Beneath the sheets, they were warm and cozy...and deliciously wicked too.

Oh yes, *wicked* was exactly the way she wanted to begin their first morning together as husband and wife. All it took was one small shift of her hips for Smith's erection to slide against her slick heat. Another roll of her hips to have him groaning his pleasure against her hair.

The next thing she knew, he was thrusting deep as the lazy morning gave way to lust, to the best kind of greed. She arched back harder into him even as he gripped her hips to pull her more tightly to him with each stroke.

How had she lived without Smith for as long as she had?

But the answer didn't matter. All that mattered was that they had each other now.

"Valentina." Her name was muffled against her hair and by the raw need in his voice. "I love you. So damned much."

She would have said it back. Would have shouted the three little words from the rafters. But before she could so much as part her lips, her climax—and Smith's—shot through her, beauty and bliss and world-rocking ecstasy taking her over from head to toe. Their mouths found each other over her shoulder again as they continued to climb higher and higher, long after they'd jumped together from the peak.

* * *

"I have a gift for you," Valentina said.

Smith never wanted to let her go. Especially not when her naked limbs were wrapped around his, her skin warm and flushed from their lovemaking. But when she looked at him like this, with a wide, almost impish smile, he couldn't deny her anything. Heck, regardless of her expression, he'd always move the sun, the stars, and the moon to give her everything she desired.

"You've already given me the best gift I could ever ask for," he replied. When she raised her eyebrows, he laughed, pulling her back in for another kiss. "Making love with you is always a mind-blowingly good gift. But I'm talking about this." He held up her left hand and ran his fingertip over the bands on her ring finger. "And especially this." He moved his hand to her heart. "I don't need anything else. Only you."

Her mouth was warm and soft against his. "Maybe just one more thing," she said with a grin as she moved, naked and stunningly gorgeous, from the bed. "It's in my suitcase." Which they'd never gotten around to bringing into the bedroom from the living room, given that they'd been too busy tearing off each other's clothes.

Cassie had left them new his-and-hers robes to wear—he really was going to have to find an appropriately extravagant way to thank his cousin for doing all of this for them—and Valentina threw him his, then slipped hers on. Biting back a sigh at having her cover up all that lovely skin, he got out of bed and put on his robe as well.

His cousin had also left a pre-programmed coffee maker, which currently had a full, steaming pot waiting for them. While he poured them both a cup, Valentina unzipped her suitcase.

"It looks like I wasn't the only one with an extra gift." She lifted out two wrapped boxes, one small, one large. "My mother and sister must have slipped these into my bag during the reception. How about we open Tatiana's first? Do you want to do the honors?"

He brought over her mug, handing it to her when she gave him the present. Tatiana was not only one of Smith's most talented co-stars, she was also engaged to his cousin Ian, a Seattle-based billionaire. Valentina had a great relationship with her sister, but things were more complicated between her and their mother. Fortunately, during the past couple of years, the two of them had grown closer.

Judging by the size of the present and the sound it made when he shook it slightly, he had a pretty good idea of what was inside. By the smile playing on Valentina's face, he figured she did too.

Just as he'd expected, beneath the wrapping was a puzzle—something he and Valentina had loved doing together since the beginning of their relationship. But what had a surprised gasp sounding from her lips was the photo that the puzzle had been made from.

The night before their surprise wedding at Summer Lake—barely twenty-four hours ago—they'd gathered everyone in the family together for a photo. Sullivans from around the world made quite a large and unruly group, he thought with a grin as he looked at his brothers, sisters, cousins, aunts, uncles, and all the little kids crammed in together so that they'd fit into the wide-angle frame.

Smith and Valentina were in the center of the photo with his mother, Mary, between them. The lake was the perfect backdrop—and he chuckled as he remembered how everyone under the age of ten had shot away from the group like bullets the second the photographer said he was confident he had the shot.

"How did Tatiana manage to get this made into a puzzle overnight?"

"Your sister learned from the best," he said as he took in Valentina's joy.

"I loved being a big sister so much, I always longed for more siblings." But her father had passed away before that could happen. "Being a part of your family means so much to me."

"They all adore you too." He put the puzzle on the kitchen island and pulled her into his arms for a kiss.

Too soon, she was moving away to open the gift from her mother. "It was really nice of my mom to give us a little special something too," she said as she unwrapped it. Her cheeks flushed once she saw what was inside. "It's bubble bath."

Taking the package from her, he read the label out loud. "*Sexy* bubble bath *for two*."

Despite the fact that they'd just come into the kitchen from making love this morning—on the heels of their wild lovemaking the night before—her flush grew hotter. "She means well."

He slid his fingers through hers and lifted them to his lips. "She really does." This was better than the edible panties she'd given Valentina for her birthday, thankfully. But since he knew that Valentina was still more than a little uncomfortable with her mother's borderline inappropriate gifts, he put the bubble bath on the counter and looked over at her suitcase. "You said there's one more inside your bag for me?"

A few moments later, she handed it to him. Smith had no idea what was inside, but it was sure to be good. After all, no one knew him as well as Valentina. He'd opened up to her in ways he never had with anyone else—his flaws, his fears, his convictions, his hopes, his dreams. Everything that made him who he was.

Once he had the wrapping off, he found a beautifully decorated cake tin beneath. "This looks like Cassie's work." His cousin wasn't just an artist with sugar, she was also brilliant with pen and paint. It was why even her packaging blew people away.

"It is." Valentina smiled. "We really owe her big time for everything she's done for us."

"I was thinking the same thing." But they'd figure out how to wow his cousin later. Right now, he wanted to give his full attention to his wife.

Savoring the anticipation, he slowly opened the container...and found the sweetest thing in the world waiting for him.

"I love it." There were a million other things he wanted to say, but for the moment, he had no other words.

Back when he'd been desperate to convince Valentina that they should be together, he'd learned that she was interested in touring the famous Alcatraz prison near the Golden Gate Bridge in San Francisco. While he didn't usually throw his name and fame around, he'd been very glad for it when he'd been able to wrangle two tickets for a private tour. He'd also arranged for a romantic white-tablecloth dinner on the shore. For dessert, he'd risked having two cupcakes made—one with a picture made of frosting where he was standing behind prison bars, holding on to them with a pleading look on his face, and a second where Valentina had been drawn with frosting, the key to the lock dangling from her fingers.

Thank God, she'd loved the cupcakes. Loved them so much that she'd broken her vow not to be with him and kissed him. This morning, Valentina had brought those cupcakes full circle.

Instead of two cakes, she'd given him one over-sized cupcake. Inside a big red heart, the two of them were pictured in frosting, gazing into each other's eyes, their hands linked.

"I'll never forget how sweet you were that night at Alcatraz," she said. "No one had ever done something like that for me. No one had ever cared enough. Not until you."

Carefully balancing the cupcake tin in one hand, he threaded the fingers of the other into her hair and kissed her.

When they finally drew back, they both looked more carefully at the cupcake. Cassie's work really was exceptional, and Smith made a mental note for an upcoming film they had going into production soon.

Her sweet treats would be perfect for one of the characters who worked in a candy store.

"It's almost too pretty to eat," Valentina said.

But Smith knew the cupcake didn't stand a chance against her love for sugar. "Actually, I think it's the perfect breakfast for the first morning of our honeymoon. I'll grab my phone and after we take a picture, I say we devour it."

"Good plan." She ran her fingers through his hair. "And then once we've replenished our energy levels, I say we devour each other again."

After carefully putting the cupcake on the counter, he put his hands on her waist and was about to lift her on the counter too—he'd much rather devour her *before* the cupcake—when they heard a sound outside the front door.

They both stilled. "Are you expecting someone?" she asked.

"No." And he couldn't imagine what reason Cassie would have for returning this morning, when she'd been so mortified at having still been in the cabin last night. "We're on over a hundred private acres, and there's a big rock wall at the main road where the driveway begins. If the paparazzi think they can follow us here and trespass on to private property during our honeymoon, they're about to find out just how wrong they are."

"Smith." Valentina stopped him from tearing over to the front door with her hands over his. "Whoever is out there, it's going to be okay."

Damn it, he wanted this to be the perfect honeymoon for her. She put up with so much because of his job, his fame. For seven days, was it too much to ask for a reprieve from all of that?

"Don't worry, I'll keep my cool," he promised. But his hands were already flexing into fists as he headed for the door.

Looking through the peephole, all he saw was the woods. "There's no one out here."

But just as he said it, the sound came again. A scratching sound, along with a little whine.

Valentina rushed over as he opened the door...where a medium-sized black and white dog of indeterminable breed sat on the front step, thumping its tail.

CHAPTER FIVE

Valentina immediately got down on the ground to pet the dog. The dog, of course, knew a good thing when it saw it and moved closer so that she could give it love.

Smith had always liked dogs. But his job had never been conducive to having one, because he didn't like the thought of leaving it in lengthy quarantines every time he had to work in the UK or Australia or Hawaii.

"Oh, look at you! Aren't you cute?"

Smith also got down on one knee. "He is. Or she?" He shifted to get a look at the dog's undercarriage. "Nope, definitely a he."

She laughed, but then sobered too soon. "Who do you think he belongs to? He doesn't have a collar." She looked down the long driveway. "Do you think he could have been going for a walk with his owner and gotten loose?"

Smith studied the dog more closely. For all his cuteness, he had a slightly feral look—as if he had been on his own for longer than a few hours. He also had eyes that looked partially cloudy. "Let's bring him inside and give him something to eat while I look up the local vet."

Valentina happily invited the dog in. "Let's see what we have to eat for you." As if he could understand her perfectly, the dog walked in beside her, leaning slightly against her leg as they headed for the refrigerator. "I know you might be hungry," she said in a gentle voice as she pulled out a container of cold cuts, "but I don't want you to get sick on human food." After he sniffed, then gobbled down the few pieces she handed him, she said, "Smith, we should get him some actual dog food."

He nodded, but at the same time he knew that if the vet found a chip, he'd be going straight home to his owner. And there would be no need for dog food.

Smith had been longing for a week alone with his new wife. But watching her with the stray dog made something ache inside his chest. They'd talked of having a family, of course, but once they'd started their production company things had taken off to such a high level that there had barely been time to breathe.

Maybe this week should be the start of something new. Not just seven days and nights of blissful alone time, not only their first week as husband and wife, but the beginning of the part of their lives where work didn't always come first, no matter how exciting the projects.

"I'll bet your owners are worried sick about you." She ruffled the fur on the top of the dog's head. That was when Smith saw her notice the dog's eyes. "We really should find a vet soon. His eyes are kind of cloudy."

"It looks like he might have partial vision loss. Although," he added with a small smile, "he was certainly able to follow you toward the fridge with no problem. Why don't you hop into the shower while I call the vet I found on my phone to let them know we'll be coming straight in?"

She nodded, then turned to the dog. "I'll be right back. Don't worry about a thing, we'll take good care of you until we can get you home."

Smith made the call, then made a clicking sound to see if the dog would respond. It was a clear path from the fridge to where Smith was standing, and though the dog headed straight for him, he was more careful walking through the house than other dogs might have been.

"She's already lost her heart to you, you know." He could have sworn the dog nodded. "I honestly don't know whether to wish that we can get you home to your owner, or that we'll get to keep you because you don't have one anymore."

As if in reply, the dog nuzzled his hand, then rolled

over on his back for a belly rub.

"Looks like you've placed your vote." And who could blame the dog for wanting to stay with a warm, loving woman like Valentina fussing over him *and* giving him lunch meat?

Smith had hoped to share a shower with his beautiful wife, but that wasn't going to happen this morning. Taking a seat on the floor while continuing the belly scratching, he idly wondered if this dog would get along with his brother's dogs.

"Looks like you've found a new best friend." Valentina emerged from the shower in record time, already dressed but still towel drying her hair.

"He's a charmer, that's for sure." With a final belly pat, Smith got up from the floor. "I'll jump in the shower, and then we can head out for the vet." As much as he liked the dog, and had secretly always wanted one, he knew he needed to prepare her for the near certainty that they were going to have to let their furry new friend go in a matter of hours. "If they find a chip—"

"Then I'll be glad we helped him find his way back home. But if they don't know who he belongs to—"

This time, he was the one interrupting. "He's staying with us."

She dropped the towel to throw herself into his arms. "I know it will be crazy with our travel schedule, but we'll make it work."

"If we do get to keep him," he reminded them both again as he breathed in her delicious scent, "you're right. We'll figure out a way to make it work."

* * *

They'd chosen rural Maine for their honeymoon partly for the quiet beauty of the area, but mostly for the anonymity. The press would assume they should look for a movie star and his bride in the usual honeymoon destinations—Hawaii, the Italian Riviera, Paris. Not the thick woods close to the Canadian border. Cassie had helped them out by stocking the house full of food so that they wouldn't even have to go to the grocery store. It had been a foolproof plan.

Of course, the second they walked into the vet's office, their brilliant plan to stay completely undercover and out of sight for a week was blown to smithereens.

"*Oh my God!*" The young woman at the reception desk nearly fell off her chair. "Are you...? Could you really be...?"

Smith smiled as he walked over with his hand outstretched. "Great to meet you—" He looked at her name tag. "—Amy."

"I can't believe you're you. I mean," she fumbled, "that you're really here! I was just reading about your secret wedding in my magazine." She pointed to one of the weekly gossip magazines on her desk.

Smith quickly noted that he and Valentina were on the cover, before saying, "This is my wife, Valentina."

"Oh...wow..." The girl's eyes were big as she shook Valentina's hand. "You're *beautiful*."

"That's very nice of you," Valentina said with a smile. She gestured to the dog, who was leaning against her leg. "We found this charming fellow on our doorstep this morning. He doesn't have a collar on, so we were hoping the vet could tell us if he's chipped. We'd also like the vet to look at his eyes, which seem a little cloudy."

Finally noticing the dog, the woman nodded. "Sure. She's in with a patient right now, but I'll let her know you're waiting to see her."

Fortunately, there was no one else in the waiting room. The fewer people who saw them, the better. Especially given that they were already on the cover of a magazine barely twenty-four hours after their wedding.

Ten minutes later, a woman with a cat in her arms walked out, the vet following at her heels. "I'm Dr. Coggin," she said as she introduced herself. Unlike her assistant, she was perfectly calm and composed. "Why don't the three of you come into my office and we'll see if we can figure out what happened to your new friend?"

"We don't know how long he's been lost," Valentina said as the vet began a quick examination of the dog's body, checking for possible injuries. "We heard him scratching at the front door this morning. Our cabin doesn't have any dog food, so I gave him a few cold cuts, which he was very happy to have. But I didn't want him to get sick from eating the wrong food, so he might still be hungry."

The vet pulled a dog bone out of a nearby container and offered it on an open palm. He sniffed it, then took it into his mouth. "Aren't you polite?" Dr. Coggin looked up at them. "And from what I can tell—and I'd have to do more tests to be completely sure—it seems that he was born partially blind, rather than it being due to a recent injury or infection."

"He gets around really well," Valentina told her. "But I'm still so thankful that he didn't get hit by a car before he found us."

"I am too," the vet agreed. "The good news is that he seems to be in perfect health. A little underweight, perhaps, but otherwise fit as a fiddle. Now, I haven't felt a chip anywhere on him, but let's see if there's one hiding beneath his fur."

From a drawer, she took out a scanner, and the dog thumped his tail as she ran it over him, head to toe.

Valentina squeezed Smith's hand tightly, and he knew exactly what she was hoping for. Because for all that he'd wanted a perfect, private honeymoon for two, now he was hoping to add a third.

"No chip. He might be lost," the vet said, "but since I haven't seen any posters up or gotten any calls, odds are that he was turned loose by people who found it too difficult to take care of him. Probably just drove into a remote area, put him outside, and drove away."

"That's horrible!" Valentina was outraged as she stroked the dog's head. His eyes all but rolled back in his head with pleasure.

"It is," the vet agreed, "but I see it happen all the time, unfortunately."

"What are our options?" Smith asked.

"There's a good shelter in Bar Harbor. But that can be pretty iffy for a dog who has trouble seeing. Especially because he's not a puppy anymore. Probably close to seven or eight, given the wear on his teeth. Other than that, I might be able to find a family to foster him for a little while in the hopes that they fall in love with him and keep him despite the extra work he'd be."

Smith shared a quick look with Valentina. "We'd like to adopt him."

"You would?" The vet looked a little stunned.

"He's exactly the dog we've been looking for," Valentina told her.

"But aren't you on your honeymoon?" The woman put her hands over her mouth. Though she'd been totally professional throughout, and hadn't made even one comment about their wedding or Smith's movie roles, at the moment it was as if she couldn't believe a movie star and his glamorous wife could possibly be interested in adopting a stray, half-blind dog. "I'm sorry, that's none of my business. It's just that every time I turn on my TV or computer, your wedding is all people can talk about."

"There's no need to apologize," Valentina said in a kind voice. "Although we would really appreciate it if you and your assistant wouldn't let anyone know we're in town. But we're more than happy to add a third to our honeymoon." She scratched the dog between his ears. "In fact, we'd love to take care of whatever paperwork you need us to fill out to make it official. And it would probably be a good idea if he had a chip, wouldn't it?"

"Absolutely." The vet reached into a filing cabinet and handed them a stack of papers. "You can fill these out while I take him into the back for the chip. Don't worry," she said to the dog, "I'll make sure it doesn't hurt." She looked back at them before she guided him out of the examination room. "You're going to have to put down a name for him on the license. It can be temporary and you can change it later, but the field can't be left blank."

When Smith and Valentina were alone again, she moved into his arms. "I'm so happy."

"I am too."

And not just because he was finally getting the dog he'd secretly wanted for so long. Anything that put a smile this big on Valentina's face was worth it a million times over. He wasn't naïve enough to think that having an older dog with vision problems was going to be easy, but they did have one heck of a brilliant dog training sister-in-law in Heather to help them out when they needed guidance.

"So," Valentina said as they split up the paperwork and both filled out the pages in front of them. "What do you think we should call him?"

Smith laughed out loud at the name that popped into his head. "You're going to think I'm nuts."

"What could be more nuts than Cuddles?" Valentina wanted to know.

Cuddles was the name of Smith's brother Zach's teacup Yorkie. He hadn't chosen it—their niece Summer had—but boy, were the rest of them ever glad she had. All of them had gotten plenty of joy over the years out of seeing his alpha, race-car-driving brother call out the name Cuddles to the dog that had him wrapped completely around her little paw.

"Do you remember that cartoon? The one where the guy had trouble seeing? They made a movie out of it starring Leslie Nielsen in the late nineties."

"Of course I remember." She cocked her head. "You want to call him McBarker? That's not particularly crazy."

"No." He grinned. "But Magoo is."

Her laughter rang out in the small room. "That's perfect!"

And it truly was. Even though for the rest of the day, instead of being alone and naked with each other like he had planned, their focus was on taking care of their new charge. They headed for the pet store and gave Magoo a bath in the area set up for self-serve dog washing, then bought dog food and a soft bed and a collar and leash.

When they came back to the cottage, a little damp and dirty themselves, Smith lit a fire, brought over the cupcake they hadn't yet had a chance to eat, and they curled up in front of the fire together, with Magoo between them on the couch. With a happy sigh, their new dog closed his eyes and settled in for a nap. Smith and Valentina's fingers threaded together as they held hands over his back.

Just like that, two became three. And suddenly, Smith found himself wishing for even more.

CHAPTER SIX

Valentina woke up snuggled into Smith...and Magoo.

They'd left him snoring on the couch in the living room the previous evening to sneak back into the bedroom to make love. Valentina had fallen asleep soon after, which meant Smith must have gone to let their new dog outside to take care of business before showing him the way to their bedroom. The big furball was obviously happy to ignore his new dog bed on the floor. Who could blame him when the comforter was this soft and fluffy?

After a delicious breakfast of the cinnamon rolls that Cassie had thoughtfully bought for them, they decided to take advantage of the blue skies and sunshine by heading off in the car for a hike. Valentina and Smith had always loved exploring on foot the areas they traveled to. Especially somewhere as full of natural beauty as the woods and mountains of northern Maine. Plus, it seemed like a good idea to let Magoo burn off some of his energy. Fortunately, even with partial vision, he got around great and didn't seem at all tentative about exploring new things.

They had been to Maine several times to visit Smith's family who lived here. All of his siblings and cousins from Maine to New York to Seattle were great people. She'd never dreamed of having a family this big, but she loved every second of it. Especially all the new little ones—Chase and Chloe's daughter, Emma; Gabe and Megan's daughter, Summer, and son, Logan. And she couldn't wait for the new babies to come from Heather and Zach—and Lori and Grayson, who had announced her pregnancy at the recent double wedding. *Naughty* was Lori's nickname, and it fit her perfectly. She was not only a great daughter, sister, and wife, she was also a brilliant choreographer with endless energy and enthusiasm for life. Lori was wild in all the ways Valentina had once secretly longed to be.

Now, though it was unlikely anyone would ever use the word *wild* to describe her, Smith knew the truth. Oh yes, her new husband knew *exactly* how wild she could really be.

As she clicked Magoo's leash into place on his collar and let him out of the car to happily sniff every single thing they walked past, she was aware of a new longing building up inside.

For a family of their own.

"What's going on in that beautiful mind of yours?"

She smiled at Smith. "I was just thinking how

quickly we went from two to three."

He nodded as they took the path through the trees toward the mountaintop lookout that they'd always wanted to check out but had never had the time for on any previous visit. "He's a good third," he said, just as Magoo lifted his leg to leave his mark on yet another tree. "I've been thinking about some of the changes we're going to have to make if we don't want to be leaving him with a dog sitter all the time."

"I definitely don't want that."

He tugged her close for a kiss. "I know you don't. Neither do I. Which is why I think we should open a studio in San Francisco."

She stopped so quickly that Magoo's leash went taut in her grip as he tried to keep moving uphill. "Are you saying we should turn our production company into something bigger?"

"We're ready to produce not only our films, but also some by established filmmakers we respect—and by newer talents who need to be given a shot at the big leagues."

"If we can do that near family," she said as the picture he was painting took shape inside her head, "then it's a win on every front."

"Are you game to make yet another big change? First, marrying me. Then welcoming our four-legged friend here. And now opening a San Francisco full-service film studio?"

"Yes." She threw her arms around him. "*Yes* to setting down roots close to your brothers and sister and mom. *Yes* to taking our next professional step together." She leaned back to look into his eyes. "*Yes* to everything!"

In the wake of their big decision, they were content to talk about the little things as they hiked. About Smith's memories of hiking through these mountains with his cousins when he was a kid. And then Valentina's stories of pretending with Tatiana that there were fairies living in the hollowed-out tree trunks in the park near where they'd grown up.

Soon, they were on the mountain's peak, their hike having zipped by while they talked. The blue skies had zipped past too, replaced by clouds, which marked their successful ascent to the top of the mountain with a downpour.

Laughing despite the thick drops of water that were coming down fast and furious, they motored back down the trail far more quickly than they'd made their way up. They were wearing windbreakers, but since their jackets weren't rainproof, both of them were soon wet through to their clothes.

But with Smith holding her hand, Valentina barely felt the cold. The first time he'd held her hand when they were heading to Alcatraz on their first date, he'd warmed her just as he warmed her now.

Straight through to her heart.

* * *

The hike had been great despite the rain, but now they were looking forward to getting back to their warm cabin. The rain was not only coming down in sheets, the wind was howling too.

He was beyond pleased by Valentina's reaction to his suggestion that they open a film studio in San Francisco. And not at all surprised. They both loved the opportunities they'd had to see the world, especially the far-flung corners that most tourists never even knew existed. But every time they got to come home to San Francisco, if only for a few days, it was always such a gift.

For so many years, home had been whatever town Smith was filming in. And then, when he'd met Valentina, home had been in her arms—anywhere, everywhere. It always would be, regardless of whether they ever settled in one place. But no matter the beauty of the Scottish Highlands or the lush jungles of South America or the windswept plains of Africa, the San Francisco Bay Area had always been his favorite place in the world.

And, he thought with a grin, the studio they were going to build was going to kick serious ass. Hollywood better watch out, because with Sullivan Studios, Northern California was about to make an even bigger mark in the industry than it already had with Pixar and Lucasfilm.

But a beat later, his grin fell away. A tree—a really freaking big tree—had fallen across the road.

The tiny two-lane road that was the only way back to their cabin.

He'd already hit the brakes when Valentina said, "I don't think I've ever seen a tree trunk quite that big."

Not at all pleased that his plan of heading straight back to their warm and cozy cabin to get in the shower with his naked wife so that he could soap her up all over had just been delayed for however long it would take the local road crews to deal with the tree, he pulled out his phone to call the county to let them know about it. But he didn't have a signal. Neither, unfortunately, did Valentina. And no wonder, since they were currently surrounded by hundreds of trees with huge trunks that stretched way the heck up into the sky.

This was the kind of moment where no amount of money or fame could fix things. Nature didn't care that he'd won an Academy Award—or that he was dying to get his wife home so that he could make love to her.

Smith slowly turned the car around in the driving rain. "There's got to be someone who lives around here." Despite all evidence to the contrary, since they hadn't seen another soul all afternoon or spotted any homes in the woods either.

"We'll find something," Valentina agreed. "And I'm sure Magoo is up to the adventure, aren't you?"

He barked as if he'd understood her question. And maybe, given that the dog had likely lived with only partial sight for so many years, his other senses had been honed enough that he could read people better than other dogs might.

Driving slowly through the pouring rain, they headed back toward the hiking trail, and then past it, with nary a house or restaurant or any sign of human life to be found. Until at last they saw a plume of smoke magically making its way through the rain and the trees.

As they drove up the dirt road, a log cabin appeared through the mist. Where Cassie's cabin had looked like something out of a fairy tale, this one looked more like a shack. But if there was smoke, that meant there was a fireplace. One that must have a person sitting in front of it, with a telephone they could use to call the county about the tree. This was supposed to be their perfect honeymoon. Smith wasn't about to let a minor blip like being stranded behind a massive tree get in their way.

Leaving Magoo inside the car, Smith and Valentina

got out and ran through the rain to the front door. Even that short trip was enough for them to get completely soaked all over again from head to toe.

Smith pulled Valentina against his side to try to warm her as he knocked on the door. Even now, cold and wet and stranded in the woods with nowhere else to go between the fallen tree trunk and the road that dead ended into the mountain they'd hiked up, he was amazed that he was happier than he had ever thought he could be.

Monumentally, stupendously happy.

The grin she gave him despite the fact that his first knock hadn't been answered and he'd had to knock again, harder and louder, told him that she felt exactly the same way.

Finally, the door opened to reveal a scruffy guy in flannel with a beard that needed trimming. He looked between Smith and Valentina, and his eyes got big. Really big.

"Val? What are you doing here?"

Smith had thought the man who opened the door might recognize him and Valentina, but the way he'd spoken to her wasn't the way a stranger would.

"Darrell?" She was also clearly stunned. "It's been forever."

Well, that answered Smith's question. Valentina definitely knew the guy. And if he wasn't mistaken,

Darrell had been the name of her ex-boyfriend from her early twenties.

Smith had been able to roll with his cousin interrupting their initial lovemaking on their wedding night. He'd been cheerful about hiking in the rain. Surely, he'd thought, the tree blocking the road wouldn't be that big a deal. Because he simply refused to let anything ruin their perfect week together.

But he'd never figured on Valentina's ex becoming part of their honeymoon.

CHAPTER SEVEN

Darrell invited them in, and after they'd quickly explained about the tree blocking the road, he went to call the roads department. As soon as he hung up, he told them, "They're planning to clear the tree as soon as the winds let up."

Smith looked out the window, where the rain was currently blowing sideways. "That could be hours."

"Actually," Darrell said, "with the weather and the size of the tree, they said tomorrow morning is the earliest they'll have the road cleared."

Given Smith's years on film sets where fresh problems popped up left and right from hour to hour, he not only got along with everyone, but he was also one of the calmest, most level-headed people Valentina had ever known.

But judging by the muscle jumping in his jaw and the tight grip he had on her hand, he was miles from calm. The ten miles it would take to get back to their cabin, to be precise. And Valentina couldn't shake the feeling that the two men were not going to get along at all.

The one notable exception to Smith's get-along-with-everyone rule was when he thought another man was trying to make a move on her. At which point he went a little caveman. And while having Smith lay claim to her—heart, soul, and body—was all kinds of sexy, just at this moment, it would be easier if he could just forget that she'd ever dated Darrell. It had been a million years ago and had never been anything approaching a big love. So she couldn't imagine that he'd have any interest in her all these years later.

"Do you have a chain saw?" Smith asked. "We could try cutting our way through."

Darrell shook his head. "Sorry, I don't have chain saw. After a couple of near misses with my fingers some years back, I try to keep my distance from power tools whenever possible."

"Thanks for making the call for us," she said before Smith could make any comments about her ex's lack of power tools. Smith and his brothers not only had quite the collection, they all knew how to use them like pros. "And it's nice, if unexpected, to run into you." Under other circumstances, she would have made polite conversation and caught up with her ex to find out what he'd been up to for the past ten years. His slightly messy log cabin, filled with books on every surface and clearly lacking a feminine influence, told her quite a bit already.

She'd barely finished speaking when Smith turned and headed for the door. Because he was holding her hand so tightly, she was propelled along with him.

"Thanks for your help. Good to meet you." Smith spoke the words rapid fire over his shoulder, clearly in a hurry to get the heck out of her ex's house.

But before they could leave, Darrell told them, "The road dead ends in another half mile, and I'm the only resident on this side of the mountain. Since the tree is blocking the only road into town, why don't you guys stay here tonight?"

Smith stopped, took a deep breath, then finally turned when he'd gotten himself under control. Valentina gave him a smile that said, *It's just one night. We'll be fine. Because he's harmless. And I love you. Not him. Never him.*

Their unspoken exchanges were usually foolproof. He always knew what she was saying, and she was the same with him. But this afternoon, when he didn't smile back, she wasn't sure she was getting through.

"Are you sure there's nowhere else we can go for the night?"

She nearly groaned at Smith's question.

"I'm sure," Darrell said.

She also nearly groaned at Darrell's response. Especially when he looked a little too happy about it as he shifted his gaze to her.

"It's either my place or sleeping in your car. And since I'm sure you don't want to do that, we'll have all night to catch up." His gaze lingered on her face. "Val, you're more beautiful than ever."

Smith made a sound beside her. One that sounded a whole heck of a lot like a growl.

Ignoring her ex's comment, she decided it would be best to focus on the details of their situation instead. "That's very nice of you to offer, Darrell, but there are actually three of us." She nodded out toward the driveway. "Our dog is in the car."

"Bring him in. I'll get you some dry clothes to change into and grab us all some beers." He shot Smith a look. "You drink beer, don't you? Because I'm all out of champagne at the moment."

Smith bared his teeth in the faintest approximation of a smile that Valentina had ever seen. "I do."

"Fantastic." The more irritated Smith got, the happier Darrell seemed. "I'll also see if I can find some sheets for the pull-out couch in my office."

Valentina almost started laughing. The very last thing she'd ever expected on her honeymoon was to end up sleeping on a pull-out couch in her ex's log cabin. "Great," she said with forced cheer. "We'll go grab our dog from the car."

This time she was the one pulling Smith outside

with her. Since they were both already soaked, she figured having a quick conversation about their situation in the middle of a rainstorm wasn't that big a deal. They couldn't get any wetter at this point.

"I love you." It was the most important thing she needed Smith to know. To remember, no matter the circumstances.

"I love you too." And then his hands were tangling in her wet hair and he was crashing his mouth against hers. His kiss was hot. Fierce. And as possessive as it had ever been. "You're mine, Valentina. *Mine.*"

"Always. I know it sounds crazy, but I swear that even before I knew you, I was already yours. I was waiting for you."

Finally, the glimmer of a smile emerged on her husband's gorgeous face. "Every second," he said in a low voice. "Every second with you is the best one I've ever known." But when he looked back toward the cabin, that grim look moved in again. "He still wants you."

Finally, she let her laughter loose. "Darrell is harmless. He barely wanted me back when we were dating."

At the word *dating,* Smith snarled. "Then he's an idiot."

"All he cares about is writing the next great American novel." She was certain that was why he was holed up in a log cabin in the remote Maine woods. "It's just one night. Heck, maybe we can even use it for material if we ever want to write a romantic comedy script. *Honeymoon With The Ex.*"

Her heart leaped when she finally got a full-on grin. "I'll behave," Smith promised her. "But if he tries anything—"

"He won't." Her ex couldn't be stupid enough to do that, could he?

Soon, they were heading back to the cabin with Magoo between them. Darrell was waiting with a stack of clothes. "You can change into these while your clothes dry." He jerked his thumb over his shoulder. "Bathroom is just down the hall."

Valentina gave him a big smile and took the clothes that Smith hadn't yet reached for. "This is Magoo."

Darrell looked down at their dog, clearly unimpressed. "What kind of name is that?"

Okay, so he wasn't a dog person, but since he was nice enough to let them bring him inside, she decided not to take offense. "Remember the animated show *Mr. Magoo*? That's what inspired his name."

"I don't know it," he said with a shrug. "But you know I never watched TV, not even as a child." He shot a sly look at Smith before adding, "I'm not much for movies, either. Great literature has always been my focus, rather than anything commercial." The word *commercial* dripped with disdain from his lips.

"I want to get these wet clothes off you right away, Valentina," Smith said abruptly. "You don't mind if we use your shower to warm up, do you, Darrell?" Smith seemed to take special pleasure in his phrasing, as if he wanted to paint a clear picture in her ex's head. One where Smith was in charge of stripping her bare.

"Not at all," Darrell replied, "but there's probably only enough hot water for one shower."

"We've taken plenty of showers together," Smith informed him, with another one of those feral smiles. "We'll manage."

Smith was not a petty person. Not a man who believed in low blows. Then again, he'd never met one of her exes before.

With that, he drew her toward the bathroom before she could protest. Not that she would have. First of all, because having her husband take her clothes off was one of her all-time favorite things in the entire world. And second of all, because Darrell had no business knocking her movie-star husband for being a part of Hollywood. He was a brilliant actor. And producer. And director. The way Darrell had phrased his comments about *commercial* endeavors was chest beating, plain and simple.

Two people and a dog were a tight fit for the tiny bathroom. The door was barely closed behind them when Smith asked, "What the hell did you see in him?"

He made sure to pitch his voice low enough so that Darrell couldn't hear him.

"He was nice."

"Nice." Smith looked so disgusted with the entire concept of *nice* that she giggled. Even Magoo, who was rolling around on the bath mat to dry himself off, stopped to give her a distinctly unimpressed look.

"Nice can be good sometimes," she said, the small smile on her lips growing as she added, "but right now, I'd much rather you show me *wicked*."

She didn't know how he managed to strip her clothes off so fast, especially considering that the wet fabric was practically glued to her skin. He reached into the shower, turned it on, and as soon as the water was hot, tugged her inside the small stall with him.

She didn't realize how cold she'd been until they were under the hot spray. This shower was good enough that she was willing to forgive Darrell for his childish jab at Smith's profession.

But even better than the hot water was the way Smith's hands and mouth were *everywhere*.

She'd thought an overnight at her ex's house on her honeymoon would be as crazy as things were going to get. But she hadn't imagined that she and Smith would end up in his shower, making out. And perhaps she should have cared about what Darrell could hear, about what he might assume they were doing in his bathroom. But when Smith kissed her like this...

When he touched her like this...

When he told her how much he wanted her, how he couldn't get enough of her...

When he turned her so that her hands were flat on the tile and moved his hand down over her stomach to slide between her legs...

When he found her this wet, this desperate for him...

When he pressed his lips to the side of her neck and sizzles ran up and down her spine...

When he grabbed her hips in his big hands...

When he thrust into her and the pleasure was so big, so sweet, so perfect that she couldn't keep his name inside...

All she cared about was Smith and the love they'd found together. A love so big, so sexy, so full of heat and heart, that nothing else mattered.

Not even the fact that her ex was barely ten feet away in a tiny cabin with paper-thin walls while she and Smith found heaven in each other's arms.

★ ★ ★

Smith's mother, Mary, had raised him to be respectful in all situations. Particularly when someone was helping him.

But Darrell pushed every single one of Smith's buttons. Making love with Valentina in the shower had helped get his equilibrium closer to normal. Unfortunately, even after he'd rubbed her beautiful naked body dry with a towel and they'd gotten dressed, he still wasn't anywhere close to even-keeled. And it sure as hell didn't help that she was now wearing Darrell's clothes.

"I'm having a hell of a time trying to forget that he's kissed you, that you two used to be this close."

"We were *never* this close." Her words were soft but impassioned. "You just blew my mind. You *always* blow my mind, touch my heart. Being with him never did either of those things." Smith was surprised when she half-smiled and added, "Honestly, he was far more turned on by his leather-bound first edition of *The Sun Also Rises* than he was by me. He didn't even mind when I broke up with him."

"Like I said, he's an idiot."

Her half smile doubled. "Which is why you don't need to be jealous. Although it is kind of adorable." She put her arms around his neck and moved closer, her curves heating up every inch of him she touched. And everywhere she didn't too. "I've never seen you act like this before. Never seen you so possessive."

"Every time another man looks at you, I'm halfway to knocking his lights out. And because men *always* look at you, I'm constantly having to rein myself in and find increasingly deeper wells of self-control."

"You are?" She said it as if she was truly shocked that other men would look at her the way he did. She was by no means an insecure woman, but she wasn't one who put much stock in her looks either.

"Day in and day out, Valentina. You're the most beautiful, sexy, fascinating woman in the world—and there isn't a guy alive who wouldn't want to be with you. But you're *mine*." He heard himself growl the word like a Neanderthal, felt his hands tighten on her hips as he pulled her even closer, but this was his honeymoon, damn it. He refused to share his wife with anyone. Especially her ex. "And most guys have enough of a sense of self-preservation not to look at you in front of me the way he did out there."

"You're right that he doesn't have a lot of common sense." Her skin was rosy, not only from the shower, but also from his touch, his words. "You know how every time we're at an event and I start to worry, you find the best possible way to take my mind off it?" When he nodded, she said, "Maybe it would help if I gave you something else to think about every time you feel yourself boiling over and tempted to put your fist in his face."

"What's that?"

"This." She pressed her lips against his for a sizzling

hot, but far too brief, kiss. Moving away, she put her hand on the doorknob and was about to walk out when she added over her shoulder, "And the fact that you're going to get very, *very* lucky on a fold-out couch tonight."

CHAPTER EIGHT

Valentina was a genius.

Smith wasn't at all surprised that she knew precisely how to reframe things to settle him down. She'd always known his head, his heart, better than anyone else. Had always been able to reach inside of him better than his family, even.

He was still amazed, however, that she'd managed to do the impossible. She'd taken the idea of spending the night on her ex's fold-out couch from horrendous...to bursting with anticipation.

Still, he could barely hold back his grimace as they sat down to bowls of canned soup—and Darrell's shirt and pants nearly ripped at the seams. He reminded himself to be grateful for the too-small clothes and the food, given that they didn't have a single other option right now. Somehow, he needed to make polite conversation before they could get to the pull-out couch part of the evening.

Granted, Smith wasn't sure that *polite* was actually on the menu tonight, given the scowl that had been painted on Darrell's face ever since they'd stepped out of the shower. No doubt he'd guessed what they'd been up to in there.

That thought cheered Smith enough to smile as he said, "Great shower. Plenty of room in there for two." He half expected her ex to leap across the table at him.

And maybe he might have, if Valentina hadn't been so quick to say, "I'd love to know what you've been working on lately."

"Funny you should ask," Darrell said, "I was just speaking with my agent a few minutes before you knocked on my door. My first novel was just short-listed for another literary prize."

"That's great. Congratulations." She sounded truly happy for him. Because she was a wonderful, giving person.

Unlike Smith, who was still fighting the urge to wipe the smug look off the guy's face. Even Magoo was lying beneath the dining table with his head buried in his paws.

"I'm really glad to hear not only that you've pursued your passion, but that it's going so well."

"It's been a true honor to join the ranks of my literary heroes," Darrell said with what was likely supposed to be a humble smile, but which played decidedly arrogant. Especially when he added, "I had high hopes, although I never expected *The New York Times* to call it *a triumph of spirit taking flight."*

"I'd love to pick up a copy and read it," Valentina said, still smiling. "What's the title?"

"*A Swallow's Wing.*"

"I take it the bird in your story only has one wing?" Smith enjoyed the guy's death-glare more than he should have.

"That's merely an allegorical facet of the tale," her ex replied. "*A Swallow's Wing,* at its core, is a deep exploration of the dichotomy of life perceived through the lens of both existential sorrows and incandescent euphoria."

Before Smith could respond to that—or make much headway into decoding what the heck Darrell had just said—Valentina said, "Are you working on a new novel?"

"You've always understood me so well, Val," Darrell said, gazing deeply into her eyes.

Pretending not to notice his soulful stare, she gestured to the notebooks and books strewn throughout his living room. "Your research papers were a pretty good indication of what you were up to. What's your new story about?"

His expression grew even more intense as he continued to drool over her. "True love lost. Thwarted destiny." Smith guessed this was supposed to be his poetic look. A look that he guessed other women probably fell for, especially when the guy threw around artsy-sounding words with it. "The twists of fate that destroy what might have been."

"Wow."

Valentina was rarely at a loss for words. Nor was she normally this close to breaking out into laughter when she was trying to remain serious. Smith, on the other hand, wasn't about to laugh anymore. Not when it sounded like the guy had gotten the story idea from his past relationship with Valentina.

Did her ex really think she had left him because of "twists of fate," rather than because he was a complete twit?

Finally, Valentina said, "That sounds…"

"Epic, I know," Darrell finished for her. "It's going to blow my previous work out of the water. The great American novel that the world has been waiting for."

"I'll be sure to mark the release date on my calendar so that I don't miss it," Valentina said with an impressively straight face. She was doing better than Magoo, who clearly couldn't take it anymore and had left to curl up in front of the fire on the far side of the room. "Will that be soon?"

"I can't rush my muse, I'm afraid. The book will be done when it's done, much to my agent's and publisher's chagrin." He flicked a glance at Smith. "I'm sure there will be a huge bidding war for it in Hollywood."

Clearly pushed too far by that barely veiled hint that their production company should look at optioning his book, Valentina simply focused on dipping her spoon into the bowl of soup in front of her rather than continuing to smile and make small talk.

"So…" Darrell's eyes flicked to the wedding rings on Valentina's left hand. "How did you two connect?"

Valentina's smile came back as bright as the sun. "Smith hired my sister—you remember Tatiana, don't you?—to co-star in one of his movies. I used to be her manager, so I was on set with them every day."

"Valentina stole my heart, right from the first moment we met." As Smith thought back to that day when he'd been lucky enough to meet Valentina, he forgot about her ex and the guy's puppy-dog longing for her. All that mattered, all he could see, was the woman beside him. The woman who meant everything to him. Turning to face her, he said, "If I could have proposed to you that day, if there had been any chance that you would have said yes to marrying a complete stranger, I would have dropped to one knee right then and there and asked you to be mine."

Her eyes grew big. "You really would have done that? Even though we were in the middle of the meeting room, surrounded by lawyers and agents?"

"All I saw was you, Valentina."

Just as she was all he saw now, the cabin and its

inhabitant having completely faded away as he put his hands on her cheeks and drew her closer for a kiss.

A kiss that confirmed everything he'd just told her. That his love for her was boundless. That forever had begun the first time he'd set eyes on her. That he cherished every word, every touch, every moment they shared.

When they finally drew back from each other, her hazel eyes were dark with his favorite blend of love and desire.

Darrell's chair scraped loudly on the floor as he pushed back from the table. "So you're both in Hollywood?" He dropped his bowl and spoon next to the already full sink with a loud clatter.

Earlier, Smith would have gotten his back up at the way her ex was trying to act like he'd never been to a movie before. But at last, Valentina had finally managed to soothe the savage, jealous beast inside of him. Hell, if he'd been her ex, he'd be feeling petty and beat up over having let the most incredible woman in the world get away.

Deciding it was time to cut the guy some slack, Smith said, "We are," and then, "You've been so hospitable, why don't you let us wash up?" It was quite an offer actually, considering that it didn't look like Darrell had washed any dishes for several weeks and everything in the sink and on the counter was covered in a layer of greenish-brown crud. "You could tell us more about your book while we get your kitchen back in order."

"That'd be great," Darrell instantly agreed, happily launching into a reading of *A Swallow's Wing*.

With Valentina standing beside Smith at the sink while he washed and she dried, bumping her hip seductively against his as she put newly clean cups and silverware away, Smith was more than happy to listen to Darrell wax lyrical about souls nearly plunging into the abyss then miraculously soaring toward nirvana.

Over an hour later—there had been *a lot* of dirty dishes in Darrell's kitchen—Valentina stretched her arms over her head and yawned. "I'm exhausted." She spoke loudly enough for Darrell to hear her in the sitting room.

She was never going to win any Academy Awards, and Smith loved her even more for it. She simply wasn't capable of faking anything she didn't feel. But there was a pull-out couch waiting for them, and Smith didn't care if it was barely dark out. He was *beyond* ready to get even luckier than he already was with his beautiful wife.

"If you could point us to those sheets you mentioned," Smith said, "we'd be happy to get out of your hair now."

He could see her ex trying to think of a reason to

delay their bedtime. Obviously, Valentina saw the same thing, because before Darrell could protest, she said, "It's actually our honeymoon."

"Congratulations."

Poor guy was still so head over heels for Valentina that he could barely get the word out. Finally taking pity on him, Smith said, "Not many people would be so nice about putting up with newlyweds. We owe you one, Darrell. When we get back to the office, we'll talk to some people who might be interested in taking a look at your book."

The other man's eyes lit up, but he quickly tried to downplay it. "Sure." He forced a shrug. "If something works out." But there was a new spring in his step as he got them the sheets. "Sleep well."

Five minutes later, after Smith had demanded submission from the ancient pull-out couch that kept wanting to spring closed on his fingers, the sheets were on. Magoo was still snoring in front of the fire, and Smith planned to check on him later in the evening to see if he wanted to come back into the office to sleep.

But for now, it was just husband and wife. Alone again.

Finally.

CHAPTER NINE

"You're a good man, Smith Sullivan," Valentina said softly as she put her arms around him. "Willing to say anything to get us out of there. Now you've got Darrell dreaming of Hollywood blockbusters."

"It was worth it, even if I have to beg a studio to option his book. Anything to finally be alone with you." He lifted the flannel shirt over her head and tossed it into the corner. "And to get you out of these clothes." He unzipped and unbuttoned the jeans she'd been given to wear and kicked them away once they fell to the floor.

She was wearing a set of her soft gray cotton tank bra and panties, and just as he'd gone crazy for the exquisite lingerie she'd had on for their wedding night, he had the same reaction now. Cotton or lace, flannel or silk, Valentina was the most beautiful woman in the world.

"The things you do to me." He put her hand over his chest so that she could feel his heart beating a million miles an hour.

"The things I'm *about* to do to you." Her voice was husky as she made quick work of his clothes too, then took a step back to look at him. "I used to think that one day, you would take off your clothes, and I would have seen it all before and know what to expect, know how to prepare myself so that looking at you wouldn't make me tremble, wouldn't turn me to goo inside. So that I would be able to keep my breath steady." She moved closer again to run the flats of her hands over his chest. "But now I know better. It will always stun me how much I need you, how much I want you. You'll always take my breath away. I didn't even know what I was missing until you showed me."

Before he'd met Valentina, everyone thought he had everything he could ever want—fame, money, a close-knit family. But until she'd loved him, he'd been missing the most important thing of all. Marrying her had been a bigger thrill than any movie role, than any industry award could ever be. And being her husband was a privilege, an honor that he'd never take for granted.

"Should I show you again, Mrs. Sullivan?"

"I want to show *you* tonight." She took his hands in hers and led him over to the bed, then tugged him down so that he was sitting on the edge of it. "Do you know what one of my favorite things about working on our movie sets is?"

"Getting to tell stories every day?"

"That's good, but not the best." She stripped off her panties and bra, then lowered herself onto his lap so that her arms were around his neck and she was straddling him.

It was hard to get his mouth, his brain, to form coherent words with her heat surrounding him, her soft skin, her toned muscles pressing against him. But he managed to get out, "The chance to travel the world?"

She laughed softly as she nuzzled his neck. "Not that either."

"Working with such great people?"

"You're getting closer."

Damn straight, he was getting *closer* as he gripped her hips and pulled her tight against him, loving the way her breath caught and she instinctively rocked into him.

"Getting to work with you makes every day the best one I've ever had." She lowered her mouth to his ear and added, "Especially when we sneak off for quickies in the middle of the day and we have to be quiet so that no one will guess what we're doing with each other on the other side of the door."

He moved one hand from around her hip to slide it between her legs. "Things like this?"

She moaned softly. "Just like that."

"And this?" He lowered his mouth to her breasts

and drew her aroused flesh against his tongue at the same time as he slipped his fingers inside her wet heat.

"*Yes.*" She shifted so that he could shower the same attention on her other breast, while curling her hips forward so that she could take his fingers deeper. "Just like that."

Smith agreed wholeheartedly that there was something profoundly hot about needing to keep their sounds of pleasure for each other's ears only. "It isn't easy to hold it inside, is it, sweetheart?"

"It's *impossible.*" She ran her hands down his abs, so slowly that he forgot to breathe in the hopes that she'd go even lower. "You love pushing me to the edge, past the edge, until I'm nearly lost. Until I forget where we are, that someone will catch us if I call out your name. And only then do you cover my mouth with yours and kiss me."

He grinned, unrepentant. "The closer you get to the edge—"

"The hotter it is," she finished for him as she finally wrapped her hand around his erection. His head fell back, and his eyes closed at the extreme pleasure of her touch. "Tonight," she said in a low, husky voice, "it's going to be your turn to go to the edge."

"I'm nearly there already," he ground out through gritted teeth, giving self-control his best when all he wanted to do was throw his wife back onto the bed and take her.

"Not even close." Her words, her smile, her movements were all beautifully wicked as she slid from his lap, then down to her knees in front of him.

"Valentina."

It would be a miracle if he survived tonight. But he could see how much she wanted this, how she wanted to focus on his pleasure, so he vowed to keep himself together. For as long as he possibly could, given how beautiful, how sexy she was, kneeling on the floor between his legs, looking at him with such desire in her eyes, her long honey-blond hair falling in disarray over her bare breasts.

Her fingers were still curled around him as she tightened her hold, then lowered her head to lick a path of wet, perfect heat up his shaft. The flush of arousal on her skin deepened with every slick of her tongue over him, around him, telling him just how much she loved tasting him this way.

He'd vowed control, had silently sworn he'd let her have the reins, but he couldn't keep his hands from tangling in her hair. Couldn't keep from moving his hips upward, couldn't hold back a low groan of pleasure.

She'd promised to take him to the edge, but considering that one look, one kiss was already more than enough to take him there, the way she was loving him with her mouth, with her hands, had him immediately teetering over the abyss.

One that he'd be damned if he'd jump into without her.

He barely knew his own strength as he lifted her from the floor to lay her back on the bed. Moving extra slowly to keep the springs from creaking—and because he could see how hot the anticipation was making her—he prowled up and over her, taking in her hair splayed across the pillow, the unabashed lust in her eyes as she looked up at him, her lips slightly swollen from the intimate kisses she'd been giving him.

"I love the way you taste." Her hands moved from his chest, to his back, to his hips as she spoke. "I love the sounds you make when I'm touching you with my hands, with my mouth. When you're almost there, about to lose it, all because I'm loving you."

He was nearly over the edge again when he took her hands in his, threaded their fingers together, and lifted them on either side of her head.

"I never knew how little control I had until the first time we kissed," he told her. "I wanted so badly to strip away your clothes, to touch, to kiss every beautiful inch of you. To watch you come apart against me...and then start all over again. Somehow, I made myself stop. Somehow I let you walk away from me that day."

"I didn't want to walk away, Smith. I wanted to stay. I wanted to tear your clothes off too. I wanted to drop to my knees and taste you the way I just did. I wanted to love you...and know that you loved me too." She tightened her hold on his hands. "I thought I could fight gravity, but I couldn't. And I'm glad, so damned glad, that you're irresistible. Because when I think about what my life would be like without you—"

"Don't." He stopped her words with his mouth over hers. She tasted just the way she had the first time they'd kissed—like sweet spun sugar, with just a hint of exotic spice—and he craved her more every day. "Never again, Valentina."

Sounds suddenly came from outside the office door, heavy footsteps moving past. They looked at each other and grinned, co-conspirators in everything. Including super-hot, pull-out-couch sex in her ex's cabin.

They'd had dozens of sexy quickies in movie trailers and editing rooms, but tonight was different. Because they weren't just girlfriend and boyfriend, weren't fiancée and fiancé anymore.

The perfect combination of desire, joy, and love lit her eyes. "Secret sex is hotter than ever, isn't it?"

"So damned hot."

And then he began to move inside of her. Slow. Breathless. All-encompassing pleasure riding them both from head to toe, inside and out.

He was so revved up that he would have thrust fast, hard, if not for the creaking springs that would give them away. But more than that, he wanted to relish every single second with Valentina.

Every one of her heartbeats against his.

Every catch of her breath.

Every new flush of heat.

Every scratch of her nails over his skin as she slid her hands from his and wrapped them around him to pull him closer.

Every slide of her smooth skin against his as she moved beneath him, with him, until they were no longer two, but one.

One heart, one soul, as they leaped off the edge, her mouth capturing his at the exact moment that he moved to devour hers, and they came apart in each other's arms.

Sweet, secret honeymoon sex that he wouldn't trade for all the five-star hotel suites and thousand-thread-count sheets in the world.

All that truly mattered was being with Valentina. Anytime, anywhere.

CHAPTER TEN

Valentina woke up warm and safe and happy in Smith's arms—and with an ache in her ribs from the spring that had been poking into her all night long.

"Good morning." Smith smiled down at her, wide awake and handsome as sin.

"Not just good. Perfect, because I'm with you." But she couldn't hold back a grimace as she shifted away from the spring. "Although someone really should put this couch out of its misery."

Smith held out his hand. "What do you say we thank our host for his hospitality and hit the road?"

"I thought you'd never ask." She took his hand and all but leaped from the bed, intent on stripping the sheets and putting the couch back together so that they could head back to their cozy private cabin. Of course, the sight of all Smith's muscles, his extremely potent masculinity...well, it was almost enough to make a girl head back into the springs for some bruising.

Almost, she thought with a snarl at the couch.

"Agreed," Smith said on a laugh as he rubbed his

own back as if it ached.

That was when she noticed Magoo resting on a pillow in the corner. "Well, hello." His tail thumped, and she stroked the fur on his head. "Did you go get him from the living room last night, Smith?"

"He was out like a light in front of the fire, but even though Darrell was still up writing, I didn't want Magoo waking up and wondering where we were."

She left their dog to put her arms around her wonderful husband, still amazed that he was hers. "I've seen you with your younger brothers and sisters, with your cousins and nieces and nephews, so I already knew how sweet you are. But now that we have a dog..." Her throat felt tight as she laid her head against his chest. "I don't know why I'm so emotional this morning."

He put his finger beneath her chin and tipped her face up to his. "You're not the only one feeling it."

There were so many things she wanted to say to him right then, but the slamming of a door reminded her they weren't alone. Soon, she promised herself, she'd tell him that even though she was already the luckiest woman in the world to be his, to have him as hers, she wanted more.

Magoo scratched at the bedroom door, obviously ready to answer nature's call. "Looks like we're not the only ones ready to go, are we?"

Fortunately, their clothes from yesterday were dry and they were soon heading out of the room, Smith carrying the bundle of sheets.

Darrell was standing next to the coffee pot in the kitchen. "Hope I didn't keep either of you up last night. Inspiration hit me like a bolt of lightning for the screenplay of *A Swallow's Wing*. I still haven't hit the sack, actually."

This morning, Valentina wasn't even the slightest bit upset about Darrell planning for her and Smith to be his ticket to a Hollywood hit. How could she be when he'd opened his home up to his ex-girlfriend and her new husband, who couldn't keep their hands off each other despite the thin walls?

For all Darrell had put up with last night when she was pretty sure they'd forgotten to be quiet in their lovemaking, she figured they owed him a decent sized movie option at the very least. "We'll wash and dry these sheets at our cabin and get them back to you as soon as possible."

"No rush, Val. I can live without the spare set for the rest of the week." He grinned at them. "You should enjoy your honeymoon."

Funny how the promise of fame and fortune could change a person so quickly. Smith and her sister were two of the only people she knew who had never let it change them.

They said their good-byes a few minutes later, and though Smith seemed over his earlier bout with jealousy, when Valentina and Darrell hugged, Smith looked a little scowly. Which, she thought as she stepped out of her ex's arms, was just fine by her. A possessive husband made for perks like smoking hot shower sex...and a night of honeymoon passion that made her breathless all over again just remembering the way Smith had held her, kissed her, pressed her into the bed while he made love to her.

Her cheeks were hot by the time she surfaced from her very sexy thoughts. "Thanks again, Darrell." The sky was so blue, the air so still, that it was hard to imagine the rain, the winds, had ever been there at all. "We'll be in touch about your book next week." Valentina, Smith, and Magoo got into their car, and she rolled down the window to wave.

Once they were back on the main road, Smith said, "*Finally*. Just you and me—" Magoo popped his head between them and licked Smith's cheek. "I wasn't going to forget you."

"I know this wasn't the honeymoon we planned," she said as she put one hand on the dog's back and the other over Smith's hand, "but even if I had the chance to change it, I would do it all over again, just like this."

His striking blue eyes met hers as he looked away from the road for a brief moment. "I would too. I wouldn't trade one second with you." His mouth quirked up as he added, "Even if it means your ex is along for a couple of hours." They were both laughing as he turned back to the now-cleared road. "Although I'm not complaining that the tree is gone, so that we can get our perfect honeymoon back on track."

The peace, the quiet of Cassie's cabin was so different from their daily life, where they'd become so good at dodging the press. It was a real relief not to have to worry about that here in the wood—

Smith's sharp curse cut her relief short.

Cassie's driveway was a quarter of a mile up ahead...and there were dozens of black SUVs parked along the road. The standard vehicle for the paparazzi.

The photographers and journalists couldn't legally get past Cassie's tall rock wall, but as Smith drove closer, Valentina could see that there was barely enough room for them to make the turn.

They'd thought the tree and her ex had been their biggest honeymoon problem.

How wrong they'd been.

Early on in their relationship, Smith had done the one thing a Hollywood star was never supposed to do—he'd punched a photographer in the face. Not only because he wouldn't stand for anyone speaking badly about her, but also because he knew she'd never wanted the spotlight. He'd thought she was going to leave him because of it, so he'd lashed out.

Now, judging by how tightly his teeth were clenched, and the murderous look in his eyes as the photographers shot as many pictures as they possibly could through the windshield, she feared there was a good chance he'd jump out of the car to try to beat them all back.

He gunned it up the driveway, and once he'd parked, the three of them got out of the car and quickly headed inside.

"Someone we met in town must have leaked that we're here." He shot a furious glance out the front window while he spoke, even though Cassie's driveway was long enough that they couldn't see a single car or photographer. "It wouldn't have been much of a stretch for that group outside to figure out Cassie owns this cabin and guess that she lent it to us for the week. And now that we've confirmed we're here, there'll be ten times as many vultures outside by the end of the day."

"Smith," she said softly as she put her arms around him, Magoo also coming over to lean against his legs in a show of furry support, "it's okay."

"All I wanted was to give you the honeymoon of your dreams." She could see how badly he was beating himself up as he looked into her eyes. "You put up with so much all the time—crowds, spotlights, press." He stroked his fingers over her cheek, so gentle, so loving. "This was supposed to be a week away from it all."

She didn't need to get away from anything, but she knew just telling him that wouldn't be enough. "Your cousin stocked plenty of food, didn't she?"

Raising an eyebrow at her non sequitur, he said, "She did."

"Her property is plenty big enough, and private enough, for some good walks with Magoo, right?"

The faintest hint of a smile played on his lips as he said, "It is."

"Those photographers are sure going to get bored and wet out there when the storm comes rolling back in—and we never show up again—aren't they?"

He was already lifting her into his arms and carrying her back to the bedroom by the time he said, "They sure are."

"Which means we have four more days to hide away from the rest of the world. What do you think we should do with the next ninety-six hours?"

She was expecting him to grin. To say something sexy. Instead, he drew her so close that she could feel his heart pounding just as hard and fast as hers. The intensity in his eyes completely took her breath away.

"I want to start our family, Valentina."

Tears came. Tears of joy as she kissed him. As she told him without words that she wanted the same thing. A girl with his smile, a boy with his naughty grin.

She thought she'd known what marriage would be—a vow to Smith of love, of an eternity of unconditional support, of laughter, of endless pleasure in each other's arms.

But every moment, every hour, every day, she realized that marriage was more. So deep and true and right that as they stripped each other's clothes away, as they wrapped around each other, as they climbed higher than they ever had before, she knew.

Knew that today was the day they'd start the family they both wanted so badly. Love creating love.

Smith had taught her to believe. To trust. And to dream.

Valentina couldn't wait for the adventures they would share next. But with their hands linked, their eyes locked, their bodies moving together as though they'd been made only for one another—as pleasure rose, swelled, then overflowed—only this beautiful moment, and the love they shared, mattered.

Love that was sweeter than ever.

★ ★ ★ ★ ★

For news on upcoming books, sign up for Bella Andre's New Release Newsletter:

BellaAndre.com/Newsletter

ABOUT THE AUTHOR

Having sold more than 6 million books, Bella Andre's novels have been #1 bestsellers around the world and have appeared on the *New York Times* and *USA Today* bestseller lists 32 times. She has been the #1 Ranked Author on a top 10 list that included Nora Roberts, JK Rowling, James Patterson and Steven King, and Publishers Weekly named Oak Press (the publishing company she created to publish her own books) the Fastest-Growing Independent Publisher in the US. After signing a groundbreaking 7-figure print-only deal with Harlequin MIRA, Bella's "The Sullivans" series has been released in paperback in the US, Canada, and Australia.

Known for "sensual, empowered stories enveloped in heady romance" (Publishers Weekly), her books have been Cosmopolitan Magazine "Red Hot Reads" twice and have been translated into ten languages. Winner of the Award of Excellence, The Washington Post called her "One of the top writers in America" and she has been featured by Entertainment Weekly, NPR, USA Today, Forbes, The Wall Street Journal, and TIME Magazine. A graduate of Stanford University, she has given keynote speeches at publishing conferences from Copenhagen to Berlin to San Francisco, including a standing-room-only keynote at Book Expo America in New York City.

Bella also writes the *New York Times* bestselling "Four Weddings and a Fiasco" series as Lucy Kevin. Her sweet contemporary romances also include the USA Today bestselling Walker Island series written as Lucy Kevin.

If not behind her computer, you can find her reading her favorite authors, hiking, swimming or laughing. Married with two children, Bella splits her time between the Northern California wine country and a 100 year old log cabin in the Adirondacks.

For a complete listing of books, as well as excerpts and contests, and to connect with Bella:

Sign up for Bella's newsletter:
BellaAndre.com/Newsletter

Visit Bella's website at:
www.BellaAndre.com

Follow Bella on Twitter at:
twitter.com/bellaandre

Join Bella on Facebook at:
facebook.com/bellaandrefans

Follow Bella on Instagram:
instagram.com/bellaandrebooks